STEWART'S BEST PEN

by Stephen W. Martin ★ art by Karl Newsom Edwards

CLARION BOOKS
Houghton Mifflin Harcourt

New York • Boston

Clarion Books
3 Park Avenue
New York, New York 10016

Clarion Books is an imprint of Houghton Mifflin Harcourt Publishing Company.
hmhco.com

Library of Congress Cataloging-in-Publication Data is available.
ISBN 978-0-544-86773-4
Manufactured in China
SCP 10 9 8 7 6 5 4 3 2 1
4500728299

For Lola, my stationery monster, who forgives all my ink stains —S.W.M.

To my editor, Anne Hoppe —K.N.E.

This is Stewart.

This is Craig.

They are best friends.

They met at camp last summer . . .

and have been best friends ever since!

Dear Mom,
Camp is fun,
except for the
wolves, but we
reclaimed the high
ground, so I think
we are in the clear.

They have a ton
of shared interests,
like getting autographs . . .

doodling on stuff . . .

sword fighting...

and writing ransom notes.

If you
want to see
Molly again,
bring ten
unlicked
cookies to
my room.

Sometimes they like to play pranks on each other.

And, yes, they occasionally argue.

But they are always there for each other.

Watching each other's backs.

Having a best friend is awesome! There is just one downside. . . .

Sometimes you can lose
a best friend.

"MOM!

Stewart searched far
and wide . . .

and even under the couch.

He visited all of their favorite places . . .

and some
of their
not so favorite.

Nothing.

Not even an ink spot.

The police weren't much help.

"You can borrow my pencil," said Stewart's father.

"Thanks, Dad,"
said Stewart politely,
"but I'll pass."

Stewart

was at a loss for words.

Craig,

his best friend,

his buddy, his pal,

his partner-in-crime,

was gone.

Then, a few days later . . .

Stewart recognized the writing right away.

Dear Stewart,

It's me, Craig!
I'm in JAPAN! I know, crazy, right?
I fell out of your bag on the way to
school and a nice boy named Tadashi
picked me up on his way to the airport.
Japan is super cool and the giant
monsters are really friendly. Please
write soon!!!

Craig

P.S. Don't touch
my stuff.
I will know if
you do!

From: CRAIG
JAPAN

This is Stewart,

and this is Craig.

They live very, very, very far apart . . .

but they still share everything with each other.

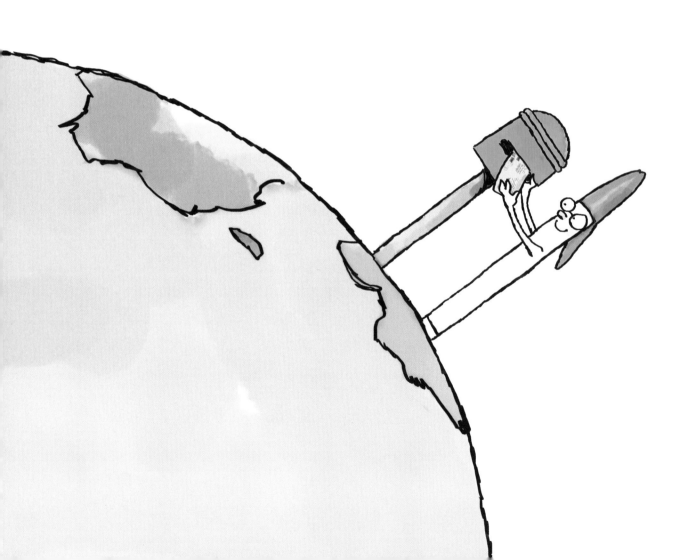

And they are still best friends,
but now they are also

pen pals!